HALL END HIGH

Gary's Story

by Mary Hooper

Illustrated by Samantha Rugen

Contents

Introduction

Miss Hogan decides to give Year 8 of Hall End High a test. Year 8 decides that she won't! Gary, Jenny, Ray and Carly put their heads together. If each of them can play a trick on Miss Hogan every Thursday until the end of term, she won't be able to give them the test.

Gary

As well as trying to work out what trick to play on Miss Hogan, Gary's also trying to work out what to do about Jenny. They've always been good mates, so would it

spoil things if he asked her out? And what would the other two have to say about it if he did?

Jenny

Jenny knows Gary likes her. She's just been waiting for him to realise it too!

Ray

Gary's best mate. He's not into going out with girls. Not yet, anyway!

Carly

She hasn't got to worry about her hoax for three whole weeks. In the meantime, she's worried about Ray. She really likes

him, but it seems he's not interested. Certainly not as interested as Gary is in Jenny ...

Chapter 1

Thursday mornings in class are usually pretty dead. But *this* Thursday was different.

I was sitting in class with Jenny.

We were waiting for Ray and Carly to come in, and laughing about something. I was thinking:

Suddenly I heard myself saying to her, "Hey, why don't you come to Mike's party on Saturday with me?"

Jenny looked up, surprised. She played with her earrings a bit. Then she just smiled and said, "OK, Gary." And that's all there was to it. Easy.

Ray and Carly came in then. We all started chatting. Well, they were chatting and I was thinking:

Oh no, what have I done? Did I really ask her out?

But before I could work out if I had,
Miss Hogan, our student teacher, came in.

"I'm going to give you a test in my
lesson this afternoon," said Miss Hogan.
"I'm telling you now so you can do some
revision at break-time."

She went out again and everyone
started moaning and saying it wasn't fair.

The four of us looked at each other
and moaned louder than anyone else.

Ray said, "That's it. I'm out of here at
lunch-time and not coming back."

"No point in that," I said. "Old Hoggy
Hogan will just give you the test next
week. These student teachers are red hot
on tests. They want to prove that they can
make you sit down and do them."

"So? I'll just bunk off next Thursday afternoon as well," Ray said. "And the next, and the next."

"She'll probably come round to your house with the test," Carly said gloomily.

I looked at them blankly. I was thinking about the test. I was also wondering if I'd have to go and call for Jenny on Saturday. The other thing on my mind was: what would Ray and Carly say when they knew that Jenny and I were … going out?

I bet this'll ruin my street cred …

Jenny pushed me. "Can't we do something, Gary?" she said. "Can't we sort of lose Hoggy for the afternoon?"

"Wassat?" I asked.

Carly pushed me on the other side.
"Can't you have one of your good ideas?"
she said. She looked at me and screwed up
her nose. "And what's wrong with you this
morning, anyway? You're all sort of
blobby."

She tapped my head with her fingers.
"Hello! Is there anyone in?"

I pulled myself together. I didn't want Carly and Ray to say that I'd changed because I was going out with Jenny. Gone *blobby*.

"Yeah. Right. One of my ideas …" I said. I stopped thinking about Jenny and whether I'd have to go in and meet her dad.

I started thinking about Hoggy and the test. "What if …" I said after a moment, "… what if we did something in class so that she couldn't give us the test?"

"What – nail up the door so she can't get in?" Ray asked.

"Something like that," I said. I thought a bit more.

"Including today, there are four Thursdays until the end of term, aren't there?"

They all nodded. "And Hoggy leaves
then," Carly put in.

"Exactly," I said. "Four Thursdays,
and four of us …"

18

"I get it," Ray said. "We each take one Thursday and stop that day's lesson."

"Right!" I said.

"But what'll we do?" Carly asked.

"That's up to you to work out," I said. "But as I got the idea, I'm going first!"

Jenny wanted to go next, then Ray. Carly said she'd take the final week. It would give her more time to think.

We slapped hands on it and hooted a bit. The rest of the class wanted to know what we were up to.

"Can't tell you," I said. "We haven't made our plans yet."

"You'll know soon," Ray said, grinning. "Just back us up when the time comes, OK?"

Chapter 2

Luckily we had a break next, so I went away to think about things.

I didn't have much time. I'd have liked to have done a really good hoax – dressed up as a school inspector maybe, and turned up just as Hoggy was going to start the test. But there was no time for anything like that.

I reckoned, though, that the first hoax of all would be easiest. At least Hoggy wouldn't be expecting anything. By the time it was Carly's turn, though, Hoggy was going to be on the look-out for trouble ...

Thoughts of Jenny kept getting in the way of the hoax.

And I still hadn't thought of anything by lunch-time. The other three kept coming up and asking what I was going to do. That didn't help.

I got my idea just before class. I rushed off to the music room and borrowed what I wanted. By sheer luck I got back into our classroom without anyone seeing me.

I sat down and Jenny came in. She grinned at me.

"I know you've thought of something," she said. "It's written all over your face."

"Who, me?" I said.

She sat beside me. "About Saturday ..." she said in a low voice.

"What?" I said in a panic. Had she changed her mind and didn't want to go? I thought quickly.

"I've told Carly," she said.

I breathed again.

"She didn't like it much."

I grinned and decided to risk a bit of bull. "Fancy me herself, does she?"

Jenny gave me a push. "Dream on. No, Carly said it's because she doesn't want the four of us to break up as mates. But I reckon it's because she wants Ray to ask her out. She's gutted because you asked me first."

"Oh," I said. Things never stayed easy for long.

"Couldn't you drop a hint to Ray? I mean, he must know that she fancies him."

"You just know those sorts of things, don't you? I mean, I realised ages ago that you … and you must have known that I …" She went a bit red. "You know what I mean."

"Oh, yeah," I said.

"So, d'you think you can say something to Ray?"

"I'll try," I said. "Maybe. I dunno. We don't ..."

Just as I was wondering what to say next, someone shouted that Hoggy was coming.

Glad to get away from the girlie talk, I jumped up and ran over to the stationery cupboard. I did what I had to and locked the door.

Chapter 3

In all the talk and fuss as Hoggy came in, we didn't hear the noise at first. Then Hoggy called out for quiet and said she was coming round with our test papers.

Ray leant across Carly and poked me in the ribs. "Where's the action, then?" he asked.

He hadn't heard the noise yet.

"Listen!" I whispered. From the stationery cupboard on the other side of the class came a steady *tick-tock-tick-tock*.

"What's that funny noise, Miss?" Ann-Marie called.

Hoggy turned round, but she couldn't work out where it was coming from. "I really don't know," she said.

We were all quiet, listening. Ann-Marie called, "It's a bomb, Miss!"

"Leave the building!" Ray yelled, winking at me.

"Now, don't be silly," Hoggy said. "Just let me …" She put her head on one side and listened.

"Please, Miss, is it a death-watch beetle?" Jenny asked. "I've seen them on the TV. They make a noise just like that!"

"Oooh-er … death-watch beetle!" Ann-Marie yelled. "They eat the wood away. The school's going to fall down!"

"Leave the building!" Ray called again.

"Nah – it's a woodpecker!" shouted someone else.

"A trapped woodpecker!" Jenny said, trying not to laugh.

"We'd better rescue him!"

"Quiet! Quiet!" Hoggy called above the noise. She opened the classroom door, looked out, closed it again. "This is most odd."

"Please, Miss, I can't possibly do a test with that noise!" Jenny said. "I have to have complete quiet for tests. I go to pieces otherwise."

"My uncle had a grandfather clock
with a loud tick just like that," Ray said.
"It was stolen by burglars last week."

"I bet they've come here and hidden it under the floorboards!" I shouted. "Shall we get some tools and take them up?"

"All of you – don't be so silly!" Hoggy cried. She tried the cupboard door. It was locked, of course.

"I saw a hypnotist on stage once!" Carly called. "He swung a watch in front of someone's face and kept saying *tick-tock-tick-tock* – just like that. The person went into a trance."

"I feel all funny!" Jenny said. "I think I'm going into a trance right now!"

"So am I!" said Carly. "I've gone light-headed." She got up and started walking down to the front of the class. She moved like a robot, in time to the ticking.

Hoggy clapped her hands. "Carly! Sit down!" she said crossly. Carly sat on the nearest chair and started moving her arms and head like a robot.

Hoggy moved back to the cupboard. "Whatever it is, it's in here," she said.

Everyone started shouting:

"Who has the key to this cupboard?" Hoggy asked sternly.

I put up my hand and said, "The school secretary." Only Jenny heard me add in a whisper, "And me."

"Very well, then. Ann-Marie, please go and get the spare key from the Secretary's office at once."

Ann-Marie was out of her seat really quickly. "Don't mind if I do," she said. "You lot will be blown up and I won't!"

She was ages coming back. By the time Ann-Marie arrived (waving the key) we were all having a very interesting chat with Hoggy about the actual noise that death-watch beetles made.

Hoggy broke off the very interesting chat. She opened the cupboard and brought out the mystery object. She put it on the table in front of her. "I see," she said. "A metronome."

"What's that?" Ray asked.

"You sometimes use them in music lessons," Hoggy said. "They help you keep to the beat." She looked up and down the class.

"Obviously a trick has been played on me today," she went on. "But the test will still be set. You have a whole extra week to revise in, so I expect you to be that much better. In fact, I …"

The bell for the end of the lesson went then, so we never found out in fact *what*. Ray slapped me on the back. Carly said, "Well done, Gary," and Jenny squeezed my hand.

I breathed a sigh of relief. That was me done.

This is the first of four books. The
other three tell what Ray, Carly
and Jenny did on their Thursdays.